The Cat in the Coat

ReadZone Books Limited

50 Godfrey Avenue
Twickenham
TW2 7PF
UK

First published in this edition 2014

British Library Cataloguing in Publication Data (CIP) is available
for this title.

Printed in Malta by Melita Press

ISBN 978 1 78322 140 0

Visit our website: www.readzonebooks.com

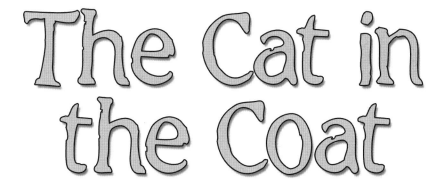

The Cat in the Coat

by Vivian French

illustrated by Alison Bartlett

READZ◉NE

A cat in a coat met
a goat in a hat.

"Mr Goat!" said the cat,
"what a very fine hat!"

"Mr Cat," said the goat,
"that's a very fine coat."

10

"Dear friend," said the cat,
"do ride in my boat."

"Is it safe?" said the goat,
"are you sure it will float?"

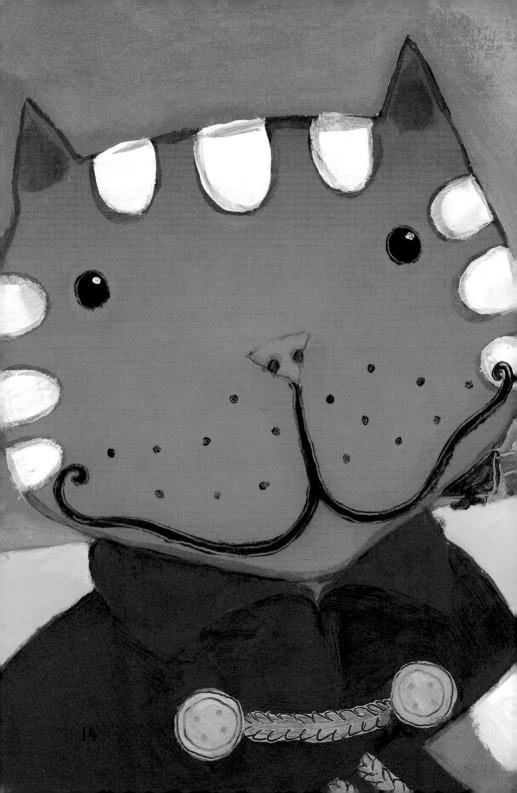

14

"Oh yes," said the cat,
"my boat is the best."

"So come for a ride —
do please come inside.
Sit down here and rest."

18

The goat made a leap and
he jumped right inside.

"What a very fine boat!
Let's go for a ride!"

But GLUG!

GLUG!
GLUG!

The little boat sank...

...and the cat made a leap
and jumped back on the bank.

And what was he wearing,
that bad little cat?

Oh yes! He was wearing
a coat AND a hat!

Did you enjoy this book?

Look out for more *Redstarts* titles – first rhyming stories

Alien Tale by Christine Moorcroft and Cinza Battistel
ISBN 978 1 78322 135 6

A Mouse in the House by Vivian French and Tim Archbold
ISBN 978 1 78322 416 6

Batty Betty's Spells by Hilary Robinson and Belinda Worsley
ISBN 978 1 78322 136 3

Croc by the Rock by Hilary Robinson and Mike Gordon
ISBN 978 1 78322 143 1

Now, Now Brown Cow! by Christine Moorcroft and Tim Archbold
ISBN 978 1 78322 132 5

Old Joe Rowan by Christine Moorcroft and Elisabeth Eudes-Pascal
ISBN 978 1 78322 138 7

Pear Under the Stairs by Christine Moorcroft and Lisa Williams
ISBN 978 1 78322 137 0

Pie in the Sky by Christine Moorcroft and Fabiano Fiorin
ISBN 978 1 78322 134 9

Pig in Love by Vivian French and Tim Archbold
ISBN 978 1 78322 142 4

Tall Story by Christine Moorcroft and Neil Boyce
ISBN 978 1 78322 141 7

The Cat in the Coat by Vivian French and Alison Bartlett
ISBN 978 1 78322 140 0

Tuva by Nick Gowar and Tone Erikson
ISBN 978 1 78322 139 4